# HOT HOT HOT

## By Tommy Donbavand
## & Steve Beckett

**Badger Publishing Limited**
**Oldmedow Road,**
**Hardwick Industrial Estate,**
**King's Lynn PE30 4JJ**

Telephone: 01438 791037
www.badgerlearning.co.uk

2 4 6 8 10 9 7 5 3 1

Hot Hot Hot!
ISBN 978-1-78464-349-2

Publisher: Susan Ross
Senior Editor: Danny Pearson
Editorial Coordinator: Claire Morgan
Illustration: Steve Beckett
Designer: Fiona Grant

# HOT HOT HOT!

## CONTENTS

Cole Day lives in the town of Shiverton with his parents, his sister, Winter, and pet dog, Jeff.

All a bit boring until, one day… *COSSSSHHH!* A stray snowball hit Cole on the back of his head!

But it wasn't just any snowball. It was a RADIOACTIVE snowball! And it turned Cole into Snow-Man – the world's chilliest superhero!

Now, whenever he munches on a raw carrot, Cole's body transforms into a big, white, fluffy man of action!

It's down to Snow-Man and his team, **THIN ICE** and **FROSTBITE**, to defeat the world's nastiest weather-changing villains.

Bad guys, you'd better freeze! SNOW-MAN is slip-sliding your way...

# CAST OF CHARACTERS

Cole

Winter

Jeff

Ray Burn

SNOW-MAN

## VOCABULARY

coconut        sunbathing
snuggled       familiar
diamond        temperature

## Chapter One

# Warm

Cole Day snuggled down on the lovely, warm couch.

He was waiting for the TV weather report to end.

Then a whole morning of cartoons would begin.

These were the best Christmas holidays ever.

"...and in the afternoon, there will be further heavy snow showers in the Shiverton area," said the weather lady. "Temperatures will fall below zero..."

Cole felt his eyelids begin to droop. If he wasn't careful, he'd fall asleep before... the... cartoooonnnnn *zzzzzzz*...

"Hey!" snapped a voice. "Wake up!"

Cole jumped, making a noise that sounded like "Jam pants!"

His mum was standing over him, and she wasn't in a very good mood.

"You've not listened to a word I've said!" Mum said.

"Yes, I have," said Cole. He pointed to the TV screen. "You said there would be heavy snow showers, and that temperatures would fall below—"

Mum grabbed the TV remote and froze the picture. She was the local weather reporter, and the family was used to seeing her on screen.

"Not *that* me!" Mum snapped. "*This* me! I told you to take Jeff out for a walk."

Cole glanced down at the dog lying next to the couch.

He looked warm and comfortable as well.

"But, the cartoons…" Cole moaned.

"…will still be here when you get back," Mum finished.

"Let Winter take him!" said Cole. "It's her turn."

"Winter is already out," said Mum. "She went to the shops to get some extra-strong chilli sauce and coconuts. I've had a new idea for a breakfast recipe!"

Thirty seconds later, Cole was wearing his coat and boots.

"Quick, boy!" he whispered to Jeff. "Let's get out of here before she starts cooking!"

## Chapter Two

# Warmer

Cole stepped outside and squinted his eyes against the glare of the morning sun.

He pulled his scarf around his neck and set off in the direction of *Big Bob's* burger van for a proper breakfast.

He listened for the crisp *crunch* sound of the snow beneath his boots.

Except, there was no crisp *crunch* sound today. It was more of a '**SPLISH**, **SPLASH**, **SPLOSH**' sound.

Cole looked around. Everything was different.

The mounds of snow had almost all disappeared.

Colourful flowers were peeking out from the grass. Buds were sprouting on trees, and the next-door neighbour was sunbathing in his garden!

"This is weird, Jeff," said Cole.

The pair hurried down the street, splashing through a river of melted snow. They saw a familiar figure up ahead.

Winter Day – Cole's younger sister – was staring up into the sky. She had a shopping bag in her hands.

"Have you been to the shops for Mum?" Cole asked.

Winter nodded silently.

"For extra-strong chilli sauce and coconuts?"

Another nod.

"You know she's going to poison us one day, don't you?"

But all Winter could say was: "Look at the sun!"

"You're not supposed to look at the sun," Cole warned her. "They told us that in science class."

"Maybe," said Winter, "but there shouldn't be *three* suns! One over there and two new ones in that direction!"

Cole blinked up at the sky. Winter was right! There were three suns! Something was very wrong.

"I think it's time for me to crunch on a carrot," he said.

## Chapter Three

# Hot

Winter, Jeff and Cole raced around the corner where they could be alone. Cole pulled a raw carrot from his coat pocket and shuddered. "I hate these things!"

Winter held up her shopping bag. "We could always nip home for breakfast…"

"Fair point," sighed Cole. He bit off a big chunk of the carrot and began to chew.

Instantly, a frozen whirlwind blew up from the pavement and wrapped itself around the trio. Icicles flashed, rain showered and snow settled at their feet.

A moment later – exactly where Cole had been – stood a white giant of a figure, dressed in a top hat and red scarf.

He had eyes as black as coal, and what remained of the carrot formed his nose.

This was **SNOW-MAN** - the world's chilliest superhero!

Standing beside **Snow-Man** were the two members of his super-team – a young girl named Thin Ice, and a dog that looked just like Jeff, only wearing an eye mask. This was Frostbite.

"**Snow-Man!**" gasped Thin Ice. "You're starting to melt!"

The tall hero raised a dripping hand to point at the two new suns. "It's the rising temperature," he explained. "Caused by whatever *that* thing is!"

The trio watched as the oddest-looking helicopter they had ever seen landed in front of them.

It was small, with a giant pair of sunglasses fixed to the front.

"There's still only one sun," said Thin Ice, "but it's being reflected twice in the mirrored lenses of those huge shades!"

"Quite so," **Snow-Man** agreed. "And there's only one villain crazy enough to build such a device."

Right on cue, the hatch of the helicopter opened and a figure emerged. He had a swollen, bald head and wore thick goggles.

"I knew it," snarled Snow-Man. "Ray Burn!"

## Chapter Four

# Hotter

"At last we meet, Snow-Man," **Ray Burn** snarled. "Hot enough, you big drip?"

Snow-Man glanced down at his body. His boots were now overflowing with melted snow. Water trickled over their tops to run away downhill.

"What are you up to?" Snow-Man demanded.

**Ray Burn** chuckled nastily. "As if I'd tell Captain Carrot-Nose my plan! It would *flood* your tiny brain!"

Then he ducked back inside his helicopter and took off again. The lenses of his big sunglasses caught the glare of the sun.

He melted more snow, adding to the river running towards the town centre.

Thin Ice pulled out her phone. "Look at this," she said. "**Ray Burn** has boasted that he's building a machine to speed up global warming. He wants to flood the whole country and turn it into a giant swimming pool."

"Flood the country?" said Snow-Man. "Just like he said his plans would flood my tiny brain! Why hasn't he finished his machine?"

Thin Ice read on. "He needs a red diamond to power it. There's only one of those in existence…"

Frostbite began to jump up and down. "**BARK! GRR! GROWL! BARK!**" he said.

"You're right, boy!" said Snow-Man. "That rare red diamond is on display in the Shiverton Museum of Really Expensive Stuff. All that melted water is heading right for it!"

"**Ray Burn** is going to flood the museum and steal the diamond!" cried Thin Ice.

"We have to stop him!" declared Snow-Man. "To the Snow-Mobile – let's go!"

Thin Ice shook her head. "We can't use the Snow-Mobile if there's no snow," she pointed out.

Snow-Man frowned. "Then how do we get down this hill in time?"

## Chapter Five

# Hottest

Snow-Man, Thin Ice and Frostbite burst into the flooded museum.

They saw **Ray Burn** stealing the red diamond from its glass case.

"Freeze!" shouted Snow-Man.

Snow-Man had whooshed down the hill on his stomach with his friends on his back.

Thin Ice had squealed with excitement all the way down.

Frostbite had stuck his hairy face in the wind, his tongue flapping around like an excited snake at a disco.

Ray Burn clutched the red gem to his chest. "Never!" he cried. "With this diamond, I can flood the whole world! You'll just be a cold memory!"

He turned and raced for the exit.

"Snow chance!" said Snow-Man as the three heroes gave chase. It wasn't easy running through the water. Ray Burn would reach his helicopter and escape before they could catch him.

"All this running has made me hungry!" said Snow-Man to Thin Ice. He pulled off his scarf. "Do you still have your shopping bag?"

Thin Ice handed over the shopping. Snow-Man wrapped a large coconut in his scarf. He spun it around his head, then let it fly.

The coconut hit **Ray Burn** on the back of his head with a

# BONK!

The villain collapsed to the ground, dropping the red diamond.

Frostbite ran forwards to collect the rare gem in his teeth.

**Ray Burn** jumped up. "I'll get you for this, **Snow-Man!**" he roared.

Fists clenched, he ran straight for the trio.

Before he could reach them, Thin Ice squeezed two tubes of extra-strong chilli sauce as hard as she could.

The fiery goo flew across the room and shot straight into the bad guy's open mouth.

**Ray Burn** sank to the floor again, clutching at his burning throat.

**Snow-Man** dragged **Ray Burn** to his feet. The criminal was soaking wet, and the extra-strong chilli sauce in his throat was causing tears to fill up his goggles.

"Hot enough, you big drip?" asked Snow-Man with a grin. "You know, you really should just chill out!"

# QUESTIONS

1. What was Cole waiting to watch on TV? *(page 6)*

2. What did Mum want Cole to do? *(page 8)*

3. What did Winter buy at the shops as well as coconuts? *(page 12)*

4. How many suns did there seem to be in the sky? *(page 13)*

5. What was on the front of **Ray Burn**'s helicopter? *(page 17)*

6. What did **Ray Burn** need to power his machine? *(page 20)*

# Stegosaurus was a large plant-eating dinosaur with a row of bony

Design: Duck Egg Blue
Managing Editor: Victoria Garrard
Design Manager: Anna Lubecka
Dinosaur Expert: Chris Jarvis

Copyright © QED Publishing 2013

First published in the UK in 2013 by
QED Publishing
A Quarto Group company
230 City Road
London EC1V 2TT

www.qed-publishing.co.uk

A catalogue record for this book is available from the British Library.

ISBN 978 1 78171 469 0

Printed in China

plates running down his back.

He lived around **150 million** years ago – many millions of years before the first humans appeared.

But just imagine if Stegosaurus was alive today! How would he cope with modern life?

# What if Stegosaurus went to the playground?

Stegosaurus would need a big friend to balance him on the see-saw. He weighed nearly 5 tonnes – that's as much as an elephant!

He might not keep up in class.
His brain was only the
size of a tangerine!

# What if Stegosaurus went on a school trip?

Stegosaurus would **always** stick with the group. Stegosaurus families lived in big herds, which kept them safe from predators.

So Stegosaurus knows it's **not safe** to wander off!

# What if Stegosaurus went for a walk?

He wouldn't fit on the pavement. At 9 metres long and 2 metres wide he's as...

BIG as a bus!

If he walked in the road he'd cause a traffic jam. He could only walk at 8 or 9 kilometres per hour – that's not much faster than you.

# What if Stegosaurus went to a party?

He could use his big, spiky tail to burst the piñata and get all the sweets!

Stegosaurus had four big

## spikes

on his tail. Each spike was as long as your arm.

And the jelly would really **wobble** when he started dancing.

Stegosaurus would weigh more than the rest of the party put together!

# What would Stegosaurus give his mum on mother's day?

Stegosaurus could use his

## sharp beak

to cut her a bunch of flowers.

# What if Stegosaurus sat on a whoopee cushion?

## Pffffffffffffffffffffffffffffft!

He'd be so embarrassed he would blush – but not in his cheeks!

Blood could rush to the **big plates** on his back.

This happened when he was **scared**, **excited** or even **embarrassed!**

# What if Stegosaurus went to the supermarket?

He could sniff out the ripest, yummiest fruit.

# What if Stegosaurus was sleepy?

Stegosaurus would probably sleep curled on his side, like elephants and other large animals do today.

zzzZZZZZZZZZZ

He might also be able to doze
while standing on all fours,
like rhinos, horses and
other animals still do.

# Stegosaurus's skeleton

Everything we know about Stegosaurus comes from fossils – skeletons that have been in the ground for thousands and thousands of years.

Scientists can look at fossils to work out how dinosaurs lived in the past.

This means we know lots about dinosaurs, even though no one has ever seen one!

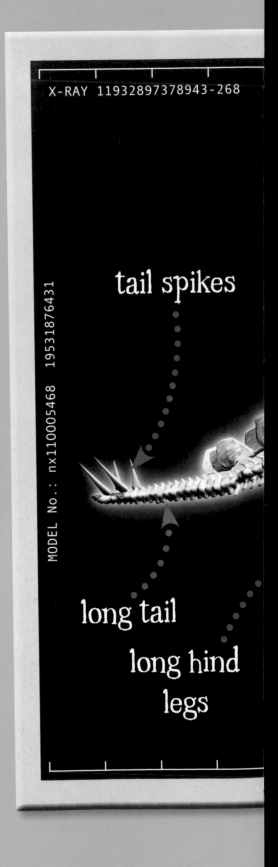

X-RAY 11932897378943-268

MODEL No.: nx110005468 19531876431

tail spikes

long tail

long hind legs

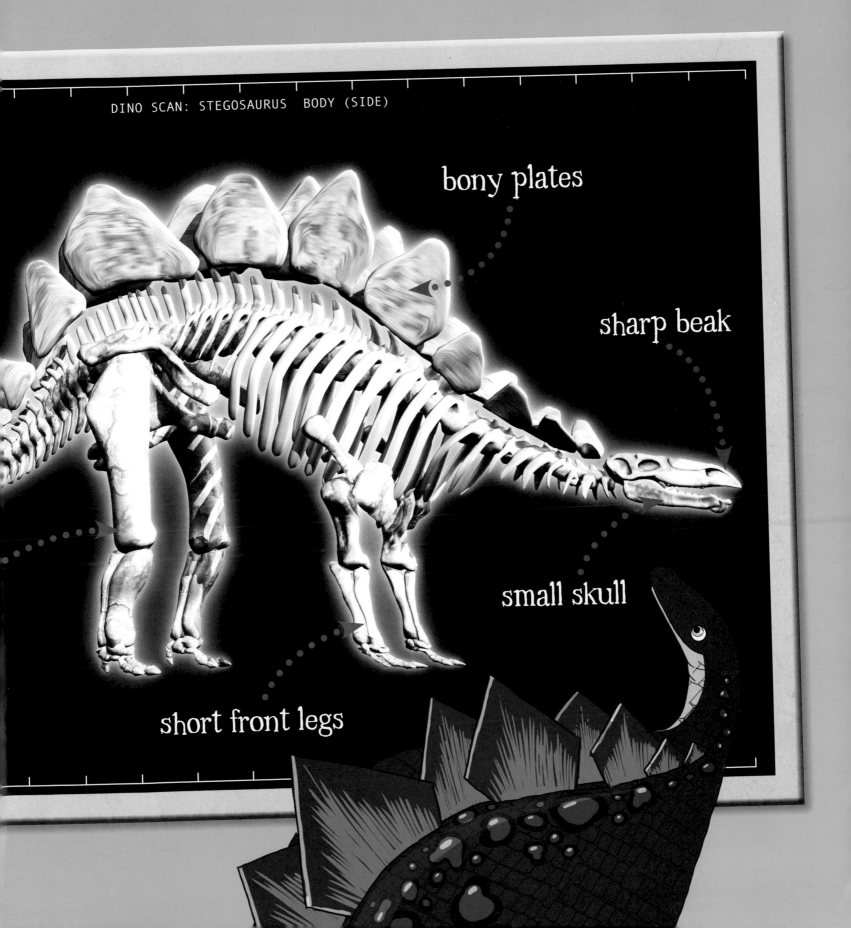

bony plates

sharp beak

small skull

short front legs

COLORADO, USA
Most complete skeleton discovered, nicknamed 'Spike' – 1992

AUSTRALIA
Fossil footprints discovered – 1995

WYOMING, USA
Back plates discovered – 1879

PORTUGAL
Partial skeleton discovered – 2006

UTAH, USA
Fossil remains found – 2010

COLORADO, USA
First skeleton found – 1876

# PASSPORT

# Stegosaurus

(STEG-OH-SORE-US)

**NAME MEANS** 'ROOF LIZARD'
SCIENTISTS ONCE THOUGHT HIS BACK
PLATES LAY FLAT, LIKE ROOF TILES.

**WEIGHT** 5 TONNES

**LENGTH** 9 METRES

**HEIGHT** 3 METRES

**HABITAT** WOODS, FOREST

**DIET** FERNS, LEAVES, PINE NEEDLES

S<STEG<<STEGOSAURUS<<<<<<<<<<<<<<<34263954302375<<<<<<<<<<48273526291083546>>>>>>>